ISBN 1 85854 379 7
Published by Brimax Books Ltd, Newmarket, England, CB8 7AU, 1996.
Printed in Spain.

Crab Island

by Lucy Kincaid Illustrated by Tom Hirst

Brimax · Newmarket · England

Storm at Sea

It was a very dark night. The stars and moon were hiding behind the clouds. The wind was beginning to blow. Soon, rain was sweeping across the sea towards the *Saucy Sue*. Lightning lit up the sky. The wind howled.

"Everyone below!" shouted the Captain.

It was very crowded below deck. The ship's cats were in a panic.

"Meow!" screeched Pod as a heavy boot trod on his tail. He dived for cover behind a barrel.

"Meow!" yowled Ginger as he was pushed from the bunk where he was trying to keep out of the way. He joined Pod behind the barrel.

"I don't know why we ever ran away to sea," wailed Ginger.

"It's getting worse!" wailed Pod.

A gust of wind hit the *Saucy Sue*. Barrels rolled and tumbled.

"Meow! Help!" Pod was being chased by a barrel!

Ginger was rolling, too! He had tucked in his legs and tail. He was rolling like a barrel himself.

When the storm passed, Pod and Ginger went on deck.

"What is that?" asked Pod, pointing to a shadow on the horizon.

"It must be an island," said Ginger.

"Let's leave the ship and swim there!" said Pod.

"Hey! You can't do that!" shouted a sailor as Pod and Ginger jumped into the sea. "Captain! Captain!"

The Captain came running.

"They'll never make it," said the Captain. He pushed a plank of wood into the sea. Pod and Ginger swam towards it and climbed aboard, thankfully.

"Good luck!" called the Captain, as they drifted away.

———— • ————

Landfall

The plank bobbed about on the sea all night. It was worse than being on a rolling ship. Dawn came. The island was a lot closer.

"Sit tight," said a voice behind them. "I'll give you a push as far as the breakers." It was a dolphin.

Suddenly, the plank was in the breakers. A wave picked it up and zoomed it towards the beach. It tipped Pod and Ginger onto the sand. There were rocks and rock pools all around. Behind the beach was a forest.

"There doesn't seem to be anyone about," said Pod.

They found a dark, shadowy cave with a smooth, sandy floor.

"We'll live here," said Ginger.

Pod and Ginger thought the island was deserted. They thought they were alone. But they were wrong.

"Strangers!" chattered the baby crab. "Strangers on the beach!"

The little crab scuttled right under Big Cyril's pincers.

"What did you say?" asked Big Cyril.

"Strangers on the beach," said the baby crab.

"We must investigate," said Big Cyril.

Pod and Ginger were having a nap. They were woken by the sound of something scratching, scuffling and sliding.

"MEOW! MEOW! MEOW!" shrieked Pod and Ginger as they saw what was making the noise.

They were surrounded on all sides by crabs with huge pincers and little, beady eyes. They were a scary sight!

"You are trespassing," said Big Cyril sternly. "This is our cave."

The crabs drew back to make a pathway to the open beach.

The cats slid between the watching crabs. "Ouch!" said Ginger.

The baby crabs couldn't resist nipping.

"Run for your life!" whispered Ginger as the crabs gave chase.

They ran back towards the forest and jumped into the middle of a prickly, scratchy bush, where the crabs couldn't follow.

"Is it safe?" asked Pod after a long wait.

"I think so," replied Ginger.

The cats had to find somewhere safe to sleep. There were far too many crabs on the beach to sleep there.

"We'll be safer inland," said Ginger. "Follow me."

The forest trees were covered with creepers. There were dark places full of shadows. Ginger walked with his tail in the air. His head was held high. Anyone watching would think that he was unafraid. But Pod could see Ginger's whiskers quivering.

Plop! Something hit the ground. Plop! There it was again.

"Ouch!" Something hit Ginger. "I'm bleeding!" he gasped.

"No you're not," said Pod. "It's juice from falling fruit."

"Falling! Falling!" squawked a voice that made them jump.
There was a sudden rush of air and flapping wings.

"It's only a parrot!" said Pod.

"Only! ONLY! ONLY A PARROT!" squawked the parrot.

The cats ran, with the squawking parrot following close behind.
At last they found a dark place where she couldn't follow.
When it was safe they crawled from their hiding place.

"We'll have to go back to the beach," said Ginger. "One of us will
have to stand guard while the other sleeps."

"We could build a cave of our own," said Ginger.

They scooped a hollow in the sand and built a wall of small rocks
around it. They laid branches across the top of it to make a roof.

"That should keep the crabs *and* the rain out," said Pod.

———— • ————

Introductions

—— · ——

"Wake up," said Pod. "It's morning."

"Any crabs out there?" asked Ginger.

They went down to the water's edge, keeping a constant look-out. There didn't seem to be any crabs about.

"We must find fresh water," said Pod.

They walked along the beach, trying the water in all the rock pools. It was far too salty to drink.

At last they found a freshwater stream running from the forest to join up with the sea. In one place it had made a pool between some rocks. They began to drink.

They didn't hear the baby crabs creeping up behind them, or see the parrot zooming out of the forest. Her wings rippled their fur.

Both cats fell head first into the pool. SPLASH!

The parrot flew up to a tree and sat laughing at them.

"Ouch!" said Ginger. Now the baby crabs were attacking!

"Wheee!" sang a baby crab, swinging on Ginger's tail.

"Hee! Hee! Hee!" laughed all the other baby crabs.

Ginger laid back his ears and growled.

The baby crab let go of Ginger's tail. All the crabs, except Big Cyril, buried themselves in the sand with just their eyes showing. Big Cyril seemed to swell to twice his normal size.

"NO growling, please!" said Big Cyril sternly.

"How does a cat get any peace around here?" growled Ginger.

He didn't frighten Big Cyril. "Why are you here? What do you want? Where have you come from?" he asked.

Pod explained as best he could. As he spoke, the crabs crept from their hiding places and came to listen.

"It looks as though you are here to stay," said Big Cyril. "But you must get used to the baby crabs nipping. They do it for fun."

"Let's show them how we play tag," laughed Pod.

"Can't catch me!" laughed a little crab.

"Oh yes I can," said Pod. But it wasn't as easy to catch a crab as he thought it would be.

"Can't catch me!" laughed Ginger, dabbing with his paw at as many crab backs as he could, before he was caught and nipped himself.

"More! More!" shouted the little crabs.

———— • ————

Treasure

—— · ——

Ginger and Pod were sitting high on a rock where the crabs couldn't reach their tails.

"We should be looking for buried treasure," said Pod.

"We'll help," said the crabs. They liked burying themselves in the sand.

It wasn't long before the beach was covered in holes.

"I've found something!" called Ginger, starting to dig more carefully.

He had uncovered something round and smooth and white.

"Be careful with that," said Big Cyril. "It's a turtle's egg."

"Why are the eggs in the sand?" asked Pod.

"To keep them safe until they hatch," said Big Cyril.

Ginger covered the egg with sand again.

"We must keep watch day and night to make sure they come to no harm," said Big Cyril.

Two nights later it was Pod and Ginger's turn for the night watch.

"Anything to report?" asked Big Cyril.

Suddenly, the sand moved. "The eggs are starting to hatch," whispered Big Cyril. All the crabs came to watch.

The gulls were gathering too.

Just after midnight, the first baby turtle wriggled out of the sand. A gull swooped towards it. It would make a tasty supper. Big Cyril snapped his pincers. The gull swooped away with an empty beak. All the grown-up crabs stood, pincers ready. As each turtle scuttled towards the sea, it had guards to protect it.

But the gulls waited. When a baby turtle began to scuttle AWAY from the sea, the gulls swooped! And so did the parrot.

She fought to keep the gulls away from the baby turtle. Feathers began to fly.

"Squawk! Help!" screeched the parrot.

Big Cyril reached up and snapped his pincers. "Leave Squawk alone!" he ordered. The gulls took no notice.

"Help me!" screeched Squawk.

The gulls gathered around Squawk. She was lost from sight.

Ginger jumped and lashed out with his claws. The gulls were cowards. They turned and fled.

Squawk fell to the ground.

"She has lost a lot of feathers," said Pod. Squawk's tail had gone and her wings were torn.

"They'll grow again," said Big Cyril.

"Did all the babies reach the sea?" asked Squawk, faintly.

"Yes they did," said Big Cyril, "thanks to you."

———— • ————

Stranded

Until Squawk's feathers grew back, she couldn't fly. Every time she hopped across the sand, the baby crabs chased her.

"Hee! Hee!" They would laugh and pretend to nip.

Squawk's feathers did grow back in time, and then it was her turn to tease.

"Can't catch us!" squealed the baby crabs, burying themselves in the sand.

Everyone knew Squawk was just teasing as she swooped towards the baby crabs. Everyone knew she wasn't really trying to catch one. But then, quite by accident, she did.

"Put me down!" squealed the frightened crab.

Squawk was taken by surprise, too. "How did I manage that?" she asked herself. She didn't know what to do next.

"Follow her!" shouted Big Cyril as Squawk flew into the forest.

Where was Squawk? Ginger spotted her high in a tree.

"WHERE IS THE BABY?" demanded Big Cyril.

And then they saw him, sitting on the branch beside Squawk.
The baby crab waved merrily. It wasn't every day he got to see the
world from the top of a tree.

Some chattering monkeys came leaping through the trees.

"What's that?" they asked, prodding the crab.

"Come down here at once!" ordered Big Cyril.

"I can't," said the little crab.

Pod had an idea. He found a large leaf.

"We'll hold it like a blanket," he said, "and he can jump into it."

"JUMP!" shouted Big Cyril to the little crab.

But the little crab wouldn't jump. It was too far!

"Push him!" shouted Pod.

"I can't do that!" shouted Squawk. "He's a baby!"

"Jump! Like this!" said one of the monkeys. He flew through the air and landed in the middle of the leaf.

"JUMP!" shouted Big Cyril. But the little crab wouldn't.

"Hold onto my leg," said Squawk. "You're going for a ride!" Squawk opened her wings and hovered over the leaf, like a dragon fly, with the baby crab dangling like an extra foot.

"Let go . . . NOW!" shouted Big Cyril.

The little crab bounced on the leaf and off onto the ground.

"Is his shell all right?" asked Squawk anxiously.

"Can't catch me!" laughed the little crab as he scuttled away.

———— • ————

Watching

—— · ——

It was a hot day. The crabs were keeping cool in the wet sand. Pod and Ginger were resting in the forest. Squawk was asleep under a leaf. Even the monkeys had stopped chattering.

"Look out! Look out!" Suddenly the monkeys were dancing about in the tree tops, shouting excitedly.

"Squawk! SQUAWK!" Squawk joined in the noise, too.

The monkeys swung through the branches. Squawk followed.

"We'd better follow, too," said Pod. "They're going to the beach."

On the beach, the crabs were standing at the water's edge.

"What is it? Has something happened?" asked Ginger.

"Can't you see it?" Squawk was pointing out to sea.

Ginger climbed onto a rock. "It's a ship!" he said.

Everyone watched. As night fell, the ship drew closer. There were lights moving about on deck. Perhaps it was a pirate ship.

"It's dropping anchor," whispered Pod, beginning to shake and shiver.

"That's no pirate ship!" gasped Ginger. "That's the *Saucy Sue!*"

Dawn came and the *Saucy Sue* showed no signs of moving.

"Perhaps they have come to look for you!" said Squawk.

"We want to stay here," said Pod and Ginger together.

There was movement on board. A boat was being lowered.

The crabs hid in the sand with just their eyes showing. The monkeys scampered back to the trees and hid under the leaves with just THEIR eyes showing. Squawk flew to the highest tree. Pod and Ginger were frozen to the spot with fright.

"Hide in the rocks!" hissed Big Cyril before he slid under the sand, and he nipped them sharply to make them move.

"Ow!" Big Cyril's nip hurt, but it broke the spell.

———— • ————

To the Rescue!

The sailors pulled their boat onto the beach. They rolled empty barrels towards the freshwater pool. When they had finished filling the barrels, they stopped to rest.

"Isn't this the island the cats swam to?" asked one sailor.

"The Captain would be glad to have them back," said the other.

"Meow!" Pod couldn't stop himself.

"Did you hear that? Those cats ARE here!"

Big Cyril crept across to where Pod and Ginger were hiding.

"Keep absolutely still and quiet," he whispered.

Pod and Ginger tried to make themselves invisible, and Big Cyril sank back into the sand.

"Why do I get the feeling we're being watched?" said one sailor.

The crabs were too quick to be caught with their eyes showing, and the monkeys pulled leaves over their heads.

Pod and Ginger had their faces pressed against the rocks and couldn't see anything. But they could feel heavy footsteps shaking the sand. Pod's breath escaped in a frightened squeak.

"They're here!" boomed a voice above their heads.

A big hand reached down and felt around the rocks. It brushed against fur.

"Got one!" cried the sailor, and he hauled Pod out into the sunlight.

Then Ginger's tail twitched and a hand grabbed him, too.

"Got the other one!" shouted the second sailor.

"MEOW! MEOW! PUT ME DOWN!" screeched Pod and Ginger.

"We'll soon have you back on board," said the sailors.

But how wrong the two sailors were.

Mangoes began to fly from the trees where the monkeys were hiding. Squawk attacked with a screech, boxing the sailors' ears. The crabs popped up from the sand and began nipping hard!

"OW! OW!" shouted the sailors, letting go of Pod and Ginger.

"Run!" shouted the first sailor. "Run for your life!"

The sailors jumped into their boat and rowed for their ship.

Pod and Ginger picked themselves up from the sand. Everybody watched as the *Saucy Sue* sailed away.

"Thank you for coming to our rescue," said Ginger.

"I hope Squawk never boxes MY ears like that!" said Pod.

"I will if I think you need it!" said Squawk, but she was smiling.

"Can't catch me!" called a little crab.

"Everything is back to normal!" sighed Big Cyril happily, as Ginger chased after the scuttling crab.

———— • ————